Ox

A Saint Bastards MC Novel

USA Today Bestselling Author

Eden Rose

Dear Reader:

Whew! I hope you are ready for this wild and hot ride. The Saint Bastards Motorcycle Club is full of alpha males with women that hang around with smart mouths.

XOXO,

Eden Rose

~ 3 ~

Ox

Prologue
Callum

It is nighttime. I have counted three night times since mommy went to sleep and I'm hungry.

I try to wake her up with my hand nudging her in the face. "Mommy, please! I'm hungry!" I cry.

My stomach is so empty and I have eaten everything in the pantries and the fridge. There isn't anything left in here.

I have gone through my mommy's room to see if she has any food in there. No food.

I go back out into the living room with my stomach hurting. There are beer cans all over the floor and her special medicine is on the table. I know it's special because she falls asleep as soon as she puts it in the spoon.

My mommy's phone is lying on the table and I grab it to call someone. I would take anyone who could bring me something to eat or drink.

My body hurts from not eating and not sleeping because I'm so hungry. I grab the phone anyways but it is dead.

I fall to the ground and cry. I know my mommy would give me a hot butt with her belt if she saw me crying. She hated crying.

I don't know what else to do. I don't know and I miss my mommy.

"See that, you dumb bitch," Tyler shouts at my mom who's passed out. "This is what happens when you do all the drugs in the house in front of your kid. Stupid whore!"

Tyler stomps out of the apartment, his dirty boots leaving dirt on the thin carpet. I cry for him to stop but he shoves me down on the ground before the door is slammed shut.

Someone knocks on the door and I run to the door hoping it is Tyler to bring me some food. I open it but see someone else.

It is a nice man wearing a police uniform. I close the door right away because mommy says the police are bad.

Chapter One

Tia

My work phone is already dinging in my purse as I scan my badge to get into the building. Reaching into my purse to grab my work phone I see that it is one of the parents who I have been trying to get ahold of. Every time I think I will be able to find them to serve them the paperwork, they disappear.

"Hello, this is Tia," I answer while pushing the door open. I have my eye on my desk in the corner in front of the window overlooking the jail. It is covered in paperwork effectively reminding me I have a lot to do today.

"Tia, this is Brenda Hager. I've seen you called a few times."

I plop everything on my desk and drop into my seat. "Yes. I've been trying to reach you regarding the summons to appear in court next week to discuss your parental rights."

I hear her groan through the line. "You know I didn't do anything. I'm completely innocent."

These are all things I hear from all of my parents. Everyone is out to get them and they are innocent.

"I'm going off of what you pled to ninety days ago when your kids first entered care," I reply politely. I'm not trying to start a fight but these are things we talk about a lot.

"I was confused. I didn't know admitting to having done meth while pregnant would get my daughter taken from me," Brenda whines.

"Brenda, your daughter was born addicted to meth. There was meth in her umbilical cord."

She scoffs. "I was at a party."

"Brenda, I have to go but how about you give me your-"

The phone line goes dead.

Placing my phone down on the desktop, I open my laptop to start going through my emails. So far, I have received the next court summons for my case that went to termination last week and about two meeting requests regarding the kids on my caseload who are juveniles.

"Tia!" Harry calls out from his office which is just around the corner from my desk.

"Good morning," I chime hopefully cheerfully.

He strolls over to my cubicle with a file in his hand with the newest foster care worker trailing behind him.

Grace has worked for our agency for about three months and has completed the training. She has shadowed me several times when I have gone out to visit my families and juveniles. My only thing about Grace is the fact she likes to get a little too belligerent with my juveniles. One time, she started to get loud with one of them who refuses to acknowledge he did anything wrong.

Grace smiles at me from around Harry's shoulders. I take the file from his hand and my heart about drops.

Sure enough, it is about a removal that happened because the mother was found dead from an overdose in a flophouse. There was a four-year-old who was hiding in the closet when the police were finally called to check on the family.

I'm happy I didn't get the removal because I like having the older kids on my caseload.

"I'm wanting you to go with Grace to try and track down the alleged father for Callum," Harry informs me.

Nodding, I look back at my desk which looks swamped with paperwork. I have three reports that are due by the end of the week before court for each of them.

"Did you already check out a car?" I ask Grace.

Since I work for my particular agency, we have the opportunity to check out a car that is maintained by the agency. I typically don't check out too many cars because I feel more comfortable in my own. However, I don't want to be riding around in my car with a coworker.

She jingles the keys in front of me. I reach over to my desk grabbing my keys, purse, phone and coffee before taking off with her.

Grace leads the way out of our office area while I tap out a text message to one of my parents to remind her to drug test.

Grace is a nice enough caseworker who is a lot older than a lot of us. She used to work for a juvenile home during the night shift before switching over to become a foster care worker.

"Which car are we taking?" I casually ask as I push the doors open to get outside.

She pushes the button a couple of times before a car flashes to tell us which one we are getting. Sometimes the bags the keys come in aren't labeled so you have to play the Dude, Where's My Car Game.

"Thanks for coming with me, Tia," Grace quips while getting into the front seat. It takes her a second to get the seat comfortable for her to sit in.

Since most of the time the passenger seats aren't sat in, I don't have to do much to make mine comfortable. "No problem. Do you know where you're going?"

She nods.

We drive in silence most of the way to the alleged father's home. That is more than fine with me as I have a bunch of emails to respond to. By the time we get there, I'm about halfway finished with the emails.

Grace pulls into a long and country-looking neighborhood with trees outlining the road. Each of the houses look older but nice enough to hide that appeal.

From a distance, I can hear a motorcycle rev up and then another. Then another.

Grace follows her GPS to the home with three men mounting their bikes. Each man is wearing a leather vest and dark blue jeans. One of them looks up from his bike to meet my eyes for several long and earth-shattering seconds. It almost seemed unprofessional how long I looked at him.

The three men watch us as Grace parks the car. I know exactly what they are thinking and what they are wanting. They want to know if we're cops and if we are, why are we here.

I pull my state badge out of my shirt to hold up in case they are needing to see if before talking.

Grace doesn't speak so I walk around the car to grab the file from her hand. I have too much to do today to sit here and wait for her to get the guts to speak.

"Is there a Brandon Owens here?" I ask while reading off the name.

The guy who was staring at me with crystal blue eyes is stepping forward. I push back my long red hair to stare at him back. There is something in the self-assured way he stands that has my attention.

"Who's askin'?"

"My name is Tia and I'm with the state. This is Grace, my colleague. We are looking for Brandon Owens. Is he here?"

"I'm not answerin' to no government names. Get off my property."

With that last statement out there, all three of the guys hop onto their bikes and peel out of the driveway.

Grace and I are left standing there trying not to choke on the dust that flew up when they ran off.

"That went well," I mutter more to myself than to Grace.

Chapter Two

Ox

What kind of state worker shows up at a biker's house throwing out government names? I don't fuckin' understand why this skirt was askin' for me.

We pull into the driveway to the clubhouse and Fat Cat nods his head from the corner of the clubhouse.

"What's up?" I call out to him while I dismount my bike.

He chuckles. "Some girl called and asked for you by your government name. I told her we don't have any Brandons here. She didn't seem to buy it. You knock someone up and not tell any of us?"

I shake my head. "Nah, man. I always wrap it up." The amount of easy pussy we have here would make anyone want to make sure they keep their cocks wrapped up like a Christmas present.

"I wouldn't be surprised if she didn't show up," Fat Cat retorts.

One of the prospects, Damon, who came with me to clean up the gutters at my house, lets out a whistle. "She was pretty hot," he nudges me.

Normally I would let that shit go, but I'm wanting to know who is looking for me. It has to be something big because *Brandon Owens* is no longer around.

Once I got started up in club life, I fell in hard. I did everything a biker is supposed to do and I'm not turning my back on that. The day I patched in was the same day I got my road name. Anyone who knows me knows me by my road name.

"I want you to go in and talk to Axel and see if he has any intel," I bark at him.

Axel is one of the guys who can hack into anyone's computer system and get the information needed. He's a crazy fucker who hauls up in his room all day with the reptiles he has as pets. I personally don't go up there.

I don't do snakes.

"On it."

Big Ben is strolling out of the clubhouse with his arm around Kendra. I'm happy these two found each other but I will tell you I'm tired of them flaunting it in my face. They are so affectionate and it's gross.

"What's up, prez?" I ask while I pull out my phone from my back pocket.

I check the screen and there are two missed calls from local numbers but none of them left a message. It wouldn't be uncommon for me to get some random calls but two from the same number is not a coincidence.

"I hear you had some chick at your house. What's up?"

Kendra giggles while rubbing her just-showing belly. This woman is the complete opposite of what I expected Big Ben to snag. With that being said, they are good together. She's about eight months pregnant and is moving slower every time I see her.

My mind is on something completely different than why some chick showed up at my house. Truthfully, my mind is completely focused on the new shipment we are getting in from Canada.

It took me a lot of fancy footwork getting those Canadian assholes to finally give me what I want. What I wanted was simple. A cheaper product that we can push to get more money in.

I know the prez is focused on Kendra and the new baby. I'm not a parent, but I can assume kids cost money. He's gonna need the money to support himself and his new family.

Plus, I would like to have some extra money in my hands.

I'm walking away from Big Ben and Kendra before they can rope me into whatever guessing game they were trying to get me to play.

As much as I try to push the skirt out of my head, I'm trying to figure out what she could have wanted as I pull into my driveway that night.

I'm the only son of one of the most infamous doctors in our state, Mitchel Owens. My father has won several awards, been honored by almost every politician trying to get his vote and many more. When I patched up with Saint Bastards MC, I had to make a decision and that was to cut my ties with my family.

I still talk to my parents who are still happily married. I, however, am not recognized as his son anymore. It should upset me a lot more than it does but I'm happy about it. That legacy is something that is too heavy for me to deal with regularly.

There is a car in the driveway when I pull my bike into my normal spot. From the haze outside, I can barely see into the car but I make out a child sitting in the backseat.

What the fuck is going on?

I knock on the window with my hand reaching behind me to grab my gun. I'm not playing any games here. The last thing I want is for this to blow up in my face- whatever it is.

The driver opens their door and outcomes the same woman from before.

"What are you doing here?" I demand while shoving my gun back into the back of my jeans.

She clears her throat. "What I was trying to say earlier is my name is Tia and I work for the state. I'm a foster care worker who is helping out the assigned worker right now. I tried speaking with you earlier."

The woman has some balls coming back to my place like this. Part of me wants to kick her off my property and the other wants to know why she's here.

My curiosity won.

"What are you doin' here?" I ask again.

"Are you Brandon Owens?"

Through gritted teeth, I nod.

"About five years ago, you were in a relationship with Megan Anderson, right?"

I about chuckle. I wasn't in a relationship with Megan. No one was in a relationship with that woman. She lived hard and blew every type of powder up her nose. She wasn't opposed to throwing her pussy at people to get more stash.

"We had relations. What does this have to do with me?"

Tia nods to whoever is in the car. The backdoor opens with a young boy coming out of it.

The little boy has thick brown hair which is shaggy around his face. His green eyes are faded because of something I don't know. However, it is when he looks at me do I realize why they are here.

This little boy is my son.

Chapter Three

Tia

My bringing Callum to Brandon's home like this is against my better judgment. Callum is a sweet little boy who doesn't understand what is happening to him but this is the only way I can get through to Brandon that he has a son.

When I left here earlier with Grace, I knew from the minute I saw Brandon, he is Callum's father. This sweet little boy is in desperate need of his father.

"Brandon, this is Callum. Callum, this is Brandon," I introduce them using their names as I'm not sure how this is going to work. If I introduce them using the familial connection, I'm worried it would backfire.

Callum's little face looks from me to Brandon. "Are you my dad?"

Brandon's eyes widen and then he nods. "Yeah, buddy, I think I am."

I stand there silently trying to process what else to say. Luckily the two guys are busy in their own little worlds of looking the other up and down trying to find out about the other.

Brandon looks at me and nods his head to the left for me to follow him. I follow him dutifully with one eye trained on Callum to make sure he is still where we left him.

"This is what you wanted to tell me earlier," he retorts.

I nod. "Yes. It has been proven by a private investigator that Callum is your son."

Brandon looks pissed. "What the fuck do you mean? A PI has been tailing me?"

I shrug. "That is not part of my concern. My concern is making sure Callum is in a safe environment and is with a family member or fictive kin."

"I want to go and get a paternity test right now."

I almost laugh. Of course, in my line of work that request isn't something I don't hear often. A lot of the punitive fathers want to make sure the child they are caring for is their actual child.

"Certainly. How about you follow us on the way to the hospital and we can get the test?" I suggest casually.

He nods.

"Callum, can you get back in your seat? We are going for a ride," I try to sound as casual as possible while talking to Callum. I don't want him to get even more stressed out than he currently is.

After the paternity test and after the results came back confirming what we already knew, I suggest we go out for dinner. I can see the stress is rolling off of Brandon in waves as he comes to terms with what all of this means.

We go to our local restaurant that has an arcade in it for Callum to play while Brandon and I have our conversation.

"I can't believe I have a son," he mutters as Callum takes the twenty from him to get tokens to play.

I nod. "He's a cool kid."

"What happened to Megan?"

"Megan overdosed in front of him about a week ago."

He shakes his head in disbelief. "I wish she would have contacted me or tried to get in touch with me. I would have tried to be there for her. I would have been there for my son."

"I know you would have."

"Where do we go from here?"

I'm purposely vague with my description of what happened to Callum's mother. I don't want Brandon to have those images in his head of what happened to Megan. I don't know what their relationship was like or if it was a one-time thing. There is no telling.

"If you are interested in taking placement of Callum, we would go to court tomorrow to discuss the placement. If you aren't, Callum would have to go to a licensed foster home."

His hand makes a fist as he considers what I'm saying. "My son isn't going to a foster home."

I nod. I'm happy he said that because I don't want Callum to go to a foster home, either. "Do you have a bed for him?"

He nods. "Yeah. Tia, I don't know what I'm doing here."

In the instant second he admitted this, I felt something swirl around my body. This isn't some dad who fell off the face of the earth when he found out he was about to be a father. This is a dad who honestly didn't he was a father.

I smile. "You'll figure it out. I have faith."

Callum comes running up to us with a big smile on his face holding a long ribbon of tickets. "Tia, look what I got!"

"Holy macro! You have like five thousand tickets!" I chant for him.

"I know!" He stops for a second and looks over at Brandon. They have a silent conversation before Brandon reaches into his wallet that is on the table and hands him a fifty. "Wow! This is the best day ever!"

My move to introduce them was definitely an iffy one, but it is working out.

Towards the end of the night, I drop Callum off at Brandon's home. I didn't feel comfortable leaving Callum with Brandon to ride on the back of his bike. I guess that is something I'm going to have to get used to.

"I'm going to need to look at your house for a second to make sure it is appropriate for Callum," I reply while awkwardly standing by the car.

I wish Grace would have been here for this part. The way Brandon is looking at me from the side is doing something funny to me. I don't know how to explain the little butterflies flying in my stomach which is totally unprofessional.

Brandon doesn't hesitate to lead us to the front door of his home. Callum is holding onto my hand as a safety net which is common for these kids needing security.

The well-lit walkway leads us to the opposing big wooden door. Brandon sticks his key in the lock, opening the door and then immediately turning off the alarm.

I slowly start to do my normal checks- making sure there aren't guns sticking out, knives littering the floor, alcohol bottles in the grasping area.

The living room looks like a typical masculine room with the giant television hanging on the wall, leather couches and a bar off to the corner.

"Can you get a gate or put looks on the cabinets for the bar area?" I ask.

Brandon nods. "Yeah, no problem."

"Can you show me the kitchen and then the room he will be staying in?" I question with an eyebrow raised.

I'm wondering if he lives with a woman. I would have thought that would be something he would have brought up... But then again, who knows.

Brandon leads us to the kitchen with a chatty Callum looking at everything around him.

"Whoah! Look at this fridge!" Callum shouts with his fist in the air.

I grin. I'm glad to see he is trying to make the best of the situation.

After the kitchen, we are led to Callum's room. The room is pretty simple with a bed in the middle, a dresser to the side and sheets on the made bed. I'm not going to lie, I'm surprised by this.

"The place looks good. Are you living with anyone else?"

"You wanna know if I got a woman?"

Jesus, the way he speaks sends shivers down my spine.

Shaking it off, I hand him my business card again before poking Callum on the shoulder. "Are you going to be okay? You can call me any time you want. You can also call Grace, too. Brandon has my number along with Grace."

Callum smiles big before running over to Brandon to grab him by the hand. "I want to see more!"

"Call me if you need anything," I mutter over my shoulder as I walk myself out of the home.

Chapter Four

Ox

Never in my life did I expect to have kids. Not after the fucked up shit that happened to me as a kid, I would never want to do that to a little one.

Yeah, I grew up rich but it was more of a burden than anything else.

What do I even do with a kid? I don't know.

Callum is a cool little dude, though. He hasn't stopped talking about how *amazeballs* the fridge is since we got here. I know his mother and I know she did a lot of drugs. I'm guessing she didn't have a fridge for Callum.

"So, Callum. What kind of stuff do you like to do? What do you like to eat?"

He smiles at me while grabbing for the remote on the table. "Can we watch anime?"

I shake my head quickly. "Um, okay."

"I like to watch TV, go out for rides when my mom would take me. I like to eat anything but I haven't had food in a couple of days before yesterday."

My heart drops into the pit of my stomach. There is no way I would turn him away.

"Dude, whatever you want to eat, let me know and I will get it for you. Do you need clothes?"

I'm becoming overwhelmed by the amount of stuff I'm going to be needing to take care of this child. I'm going to need a kid's toothbrush, clothes, underwear, socks... My brain is swimming.

I'm known for taking extreme risks at Saint Bastards but this is a whole other thing.

"How about me sit and relax tonight and then tomorrow we can get some stuff?" I ask.

"Want to watch TV with me?" Callum asks.

I smile at him and take the seat next to him. We sit in a comfortable silence until we both doze off.

When I'm startled awake by my ringing phone, I remember everything about yesterday. I'm a father. I have a child here I'm supposed to take care of.

I'm fucked.

"'lo?" I answer the phone.

"My name is Chris and I'm calling from the county. I'm looking for Brandon?"

Again with the government names. "Yeah?"

"I'm a licensing worker who is going to need to come over this week to get you to sign some paperwork. What days work best for you?"

"What kind of paperwork?" I notice Callum is resting against the back of the couch with a dreamy look on his face.

Maybe a kid won't be that bad? I have no idea.

"Standard paperwork and I have to verify your house is safe for the youth."

I nod. "Sure. I'm available today in a little bit if you want to come over."

I'm already trying to figure out what to say to the guys when I go in there with Callum. My head is swimming with all of these things that I need to do, but I can't help but wonder why Megan would have kept this a secret.

The Megan I knew back in the day would have taken every opportunity to fuck me over to get more money. Anything she could have done, she would have done it.

Fuck me.

I look down at Callum and think about the shit he could have seen while at his mom's. Megan lived a hard life and partied even harder. She wouldn't be the type who would put that away just because she is pregnant.

I reach into the pocket of my jeans to pull out Tia's number. I need help figuring out what to get Callum.

I'm flicking the business card with my fingers as I pace the kitchen. The sun is already up and it is a Friday.

I'm normally a cocky mother fucker who doesn't have to do much to get a woman's attention. With a quick grin and a head nod, they're taking off their panties for me. Tia isn't like those girls.

I dial her number and listen to it ring a couple of times before she answers. "This is Tia."

Tia has a sexy voice that does things to my body just thinking about her voice.

"Tia, this is Ox, erm, Brandon," I mutter. I hate using my government name.

I hear shuffling in the background and then a cleared throat. "Brandon, is everything all right?"

I rub the back of my neck and begin to pace a little. I'm never this much of a pussy. I also never thought I would have children. I'm the type of guy who wraps my cock up and then ties the condom to throw it away.

"I need some help on what to buy Callum. Can you help me?"

She giggles. "I take it they don't have a lot of kids in your gang?"

I let the *gang* part go. Normally I would be pissed off if someone referred to my club as a gang. "Yeah, whatever. Can you help?"

I can her smiling over the phone lines. "Yeah. I get out of work at five. Meet me at Target at five."

I hang up.

Next, I need to call Big Ben.

"Where you at, Ox?" Big Ben answers the phone.

"You will never believe who that chick was."

"Did you knock her up and you didn't know about it?"

"Asshole."

"I'm just wondering. You know how to fuck around."

I stop pacing and lean on my left arm that is resting on the countertop. "That woman was a social worker. I'm a dad."

I can hear him scoff. "What?"

"Yep. I'm meeting her today at Target at five to go over the things I need to take care of him."

"You're a dad? You sure about this?"

I take a look at my sleeping son on the couch. "Yeah. I got tested already and it came back. I need to take today off to handle this."

He chuckles. "I can't believe you have a kid. Do you need anything?"

"Uh, I don't know yet."

~ 35 ~

Chapter Five

Tia

"How'd it go last night?" Grace asks while hanging on the divider of my cubicle. "Sorry I couldn't go. I had to pick up Oliver from daycare."

Oliver is Grace's two-year-old son. Grace cuts out of work early to be with him a lot and then I have to cover her visits.

"No problem. It went well enough," I reply why shaking the mouse on my desk. "I'm going to help him pick up the kid basics he is going to need," I throw out there.

She giggles. "He's pretty cute, huh? I mean, for a scary and hairy biker."

"Sure, I guess." I'm lying through my teeth. I think he is very cute.

All last night, I was thinking about him and how he was doing with Callum. It must have been pretty shocking to find out you have a son and then an hour later, a random kid is in your home living there. I don't blame him for needing some help.

I smile at Grace and then turn back to my computer. I have a meeting in about twenty minutes with a father who is denying paternity of a daughter who looks like him.

While I'm finishing entering the contacts I made yesterday, I hear Harry approaching my cubicle. He likes to sit in on a few of my meetings to help provide guidance when needed.

"Are you ready? Dave and his attorney are in the conference room."

"Yep!" I push the power button on the computer to make it go to sleep before grabbing my pad of paper and a pen.

Sure enough, when we enter the conference room Dave and his attorney are there. I like a lot of our attorneys but I'm not a fan of this one. Kyle Horbath is a tricky lawyer who loves throwing curveballs at caseworkers.

"Good morning," I chime as I set my stuff down on the table to the left of my client and his attorney. "How are you today?"

Harry sits next to me with his coffee mug in front of him. Damn, I knew I forgot something.

"All I'm saying is I'm not doing any drug tests or doing a damn psychological evaluation. That's not my kid," Dave automatically spits.

I smile. "Dave, we've discussed that at this point the services we are offering are voluntary until the hearing next week."

Dave is a skinny guy with a crazy mohawk on his head. He is mumbling more to himself than to me as he shakes his head. "I know what you're going to do. You're going to get me locked up."

Kyle clears his throat. "Why would you get locked up?"

"Look, all I know is I didn't love Amber and we didn't have sex."

I fight my scoff. "Excuse me?"

"I didn't come in her. I don't get why I would have knocked her up."

*

By the time five o'clock hits, I want to ram my head against the desk. Things didn't get better after Dave's meeting. I have a lot of stuff that still needs to get done, but I'm leaving my computer at work.

I grab my work phone and shove it in my purse. I like to keep my work phone on me in case one of my kiddos needs something. I would hate for something bad to happen to them.

A lot of caseworkers leave their work phones at the office, though.

I stop by the bathroom on my way out to check my makeup and my hair. I knew I was going to have a long day of staring at my computer so I didn't do too much in the makeup area. I rolled some curls in my hair to make my hair look anything more than straight as a pin.

After slathering on some chapstick, I shrug in the mirror and curse myself for trying to get cute for someone that I could never be with.

All of the guys I have dated have one thing in common and that's the red flags that beam off their heads. I'm attracted to the red flags like a bull running straight towards them as quickly as I can.

I have dated a few guys who seemed normal at first. They treated me nicely, they were sweet, our passion was decent... And then it instantly switches to a Humpity Dumpty situation. I tried to fix as many as I could and it was the last guy I dated that makes me apprehensive of dating anyone again.

The last guy was named Rick and I met him at a bar about two years ago. We dated for a year, had some fun until things started to get real. I had just started my job and I realized he was using me. While I worked during the day, I would come home and find my house littered with beer bottles and dirty dishes. He didn't clean up anything while I was at work.

Then the big thing happened. I came home from work early because Rick and I got into a fight the night before about money. I felt bad for calling him a lazy loser so I wanted to make it up to him. I was expecting to surprise him but it was me who got the surprise since he was having sex with our neighbor.

You can imagine my apprehension about dating anyone.

I pull up to Target at five after which is still good timing. I can see Brandon and Callum standing at the entrance to the store. Brandon looks very uneasy in his worn-out jeans, biker boots and leather vest on.

I wasn't surprised to see Callum wearing the same clothing he wore yesterday.

I fight the urge to hug them both. That would be completely unprofessional. However, this isn't my case. I don't have any connection to it.

I keep repeating that to myself as I walk up.

"Hi, guys! How are you?" I greet them.

Callum comes running up to me throwing his arms around my waist. "Dad and me made pancakes!"

I smile. "Sounds fun! Are you ready to show your dad the things you might need?"

We are about to enter the store when a beautiful, but pregnant woman throws an arm through Brandon's arm. I'm thrown off by this. Does he have a girlfriend?

Much more than that, does he have a pregnant girlfriend?

"Kendra!" Brandon yells out in surprise. "Did Ben tell you to come fuckin' spy on me?"

Callum's nose twitches. "You said a bad word," he scolds causing us all to laugh a little.

"Get used to it, little buddy."

Kendra, also known as the beautifully pregnant woman, giggles. "Yes. I'm here to make sure you don't do anything stupid." She throws her long black hair over her shoulder then sticks her hand out for me to shake. "I'm Kendra. I'm Ben's girlfriend."

Brandon rolls his eyes. "He's gonna smack you for that connection," he tsks.

I'm surprised at the relationship between the two of them. I wouldn't have expected Brandon to be so chummy with another woman.

"Hi, I'm Tia. I'm…" I'm not exactly sure what I am right now.

"My friend," Callum answers gleefully.

Kendra walks next to us as quickly as she can which isn't quick at all. You can tell she's uncomfortable as all get out.

Callum is having a blast going through the store and helping pick out what he wants. There are a couple of times through the store, I purposely brush Brandon's hand. I don't know why I do it, but I do it anyway.

Brandon is hot in a bad-boy kind of way. He is the exact opposite of all of the losers I previously dated.

Kendra grabs me by my hand to hold me back for a second while Callum and Brandon as looking at toys. Brandon's cart is overfilled with everything and more for Callum. I can tell one thing, this is a good fit.

"So, I don't know you very well but I have to tell you, I have seen Ox smile this much," she whispers.

I fight the urge to smile. "He's going to make a great dad," I admit truthfully.

"I mean, I think you should go for it."

"Excuse me?" I blurt.

Kendra stops waddling behind her own overfilled cart to pin me with a look. "I know girls like you. I am a girl like you. I just want to say don't let the hard-candy-shell turn you off on a good man."

Chapter Six

Ox

"I don't know what I would have done without you," I admit to Tia while swiping my card.

I damn near bought the whole store! Callum is set for clothes, toys, bath stuff, shoes and two different gaming systems.

"I think you could have figured it out," she replies happily.

Kendra left about twenty minutes ago complaining about being too tired. She winked at me while she left the store with about four hundred dollars worth of stuff.

Glad she's not my woman.

"Where do you want to eat?" I ask.

She clears her throat. "Um, I'm good. Thanks. I should probably get going home."

I stop in front of her with Callum holding my hand. "I wasn't asking. Where do you want to eat?"

Tia is trying to think of a way to get out of dinner with me but I'm not taking no. I appreciate her help and honestly just want to spend time with her.

Jesus. I need to go back to the club. This chick has me all turned out.

Callum is vibrating with excitement. "We should go to the arcade!"

She raises an eyebrow and nods. "That sounds like a plan."

With Callum set up in his car seat, I see Tia making a mad dash to her own SUV. I make her nervous, I can tell that I do. What I want to know is why I'm making her so nervous.

"Tia, wait."

She stops in the middle of the parking lot then turns to look at me. "What?"

Her chest is rising causing her tits to push against the cotton of her shirt. She is beyond sexy.

"Are you afraid of me?"

She shakes her head. "That's ridiculous. I'm just here to help."

I smirk. "I think we both know you're here to do a lot more than help," I retort.

Tia doesn't respond. I didn't expect her to. I bet she didn't think I would call her out on the truth.

She knows she's here for more help.

"Dad," Callum rolls down the window calling for me.

I get a warm feeling inside when he calls me that. It's only been a day but I love it. I'm still scared shitless, but it's great.

"What?"

"We gotta go get pizza and win some stuff!"

I chuckle. "Right on, little dude."

Tia beat us to the arcade which wouldn't have happened if I didn't have Callum. I'm known for being an asshole driver.

"Well, look at this," I greet her with my signature grin.

I can tell she's visibly trying to recover from my advances. "Thanks for the invite," she replies.

"Sure."

Callum grabs us both by the hands and drags us through the door. The hostess steps in front of my excited son to stop him from barreling through the arcade.

"Just you three today, mom and dad?"

Well, fuck.

Why do I like the way that sounds? I shouldn't.

Instead of correcting her, I just nod.

"For real, you didn't have to do this," Tia states while sitting on the left side of the table.

Our conversation flows freely between the three of us. Callum is acting like I have known him his whole life. He keeps trying to tell me life stories but gets too excited then starts another story.

Tia's face could crack because she's smiling so much at Callum's silly nature. I hand him off a fifty for him to go play again.

"Tia, why are you actin' all nervous?"

Tia plays with a little chunk of her hair twirling it between her fingers. "I... look. Whatever you're trying to do, I don't want to be in the way. I can be here to support you but I'm not your caseworker and this isn't something a caseworker should be doing," she blurts.

I reach across the table to grab her hand to shut her up. "I know you're not our caseworker. Why are you so nervous?"

"I find you a little intimidating."

I can't help but chuckle at her comment. I've killed before. I live a hard life full of hard kinks. I'm not an easy man. I love living hard.

"Well, maybe you should."

My phone is ringing in my pocket pulling me away from the conversation. I look at the caller ID and see it is Big Ben.

"What's up, prez?"

"I need you to get down to the highway right now. Some fucker tried to run Nero off the road and stole the stash."

I'm looking at Tia trying to see if she heard him. I'm glad she doesn't say anything or act like she did.

"I'll be there in fifteen."

I hang up my phone and try to figure out what to say to Tia. "I have an emergency. Can I give you my key and have you take Callum back to my house?"

Without hesitation, she nods. "Yeah, sure. Whatever you need."

Maybe this girl is more of the ol' lady type than I thought.

Chapter Seven

Tia

It is after eight by the time we get back to Brandon's house. Callum hasn't stopped talking since Brandon dumped his car for his bike leaving me the keys in case I need to take the car.

I have my own, but I appreciate the offer.

"Callum, you know what we should do to help your dad out?" I ask him as I clap my hands.

He stops walking around for a second to turn his little brown eyes to me. "What?"

I smile. "We should get your stuff out of the car and start washing the clothes?" I offer. I'm trying to keep myself busy as I wait for Brandon to come back. I never would have thought I would be sitting in his house with his kid waiting for him.

Does this make me pathetic? I don't even know.

"Yeah! My mom…"

"Your mom what?" I ask. It is common for kids who have gone through a trauma to talk about their parents. I didn't think he would be willing to talk about his mother so quickly.

"I," he begins then stops. "I don't know. Let's go get my stuff. I can't wait to have stuff!"

Callum is running out the door before I can even shove my feet back into my ballet flats. He has the door yanked open with a full sprint out to the car. He has the car door open with the bags dangling from his little hands.

One thing I can tell about Callum is he is used to being the adult in his household when he lived with his mom. A lot of these kids who come from the environment Megan lived in, grow up quickly.

"Slow down there, little buddy!" I laugh before running out to help him.

Callum is too excited to even say anything. He is too busy running past me into the house to drop the bags off in the living room.

It took us three trips to bring everything in and an additional twenty minutes pulling the tags off the clothes. I remembered where the laundry was when he showed me the home so I didn't need to snoop too much.

"Want to help me put the laundry soap in?" I ask Callum who is literally vibrating with excitement.

"Yeah!"

With all of his new clothes in the washer, we sit down in front of the television to pick something to watch. I check the clock on my phone to see what time it is and realize it is after ten. I thought Brandon would have been back by now.

"Tia?"

"Yeah?"

"Where's my dad?" Callum's sweet little voice asks.

I shrug my shoulders a little. "I'm not sure. I bet he will be coming home soon."

"I don't want to go to bed until he comes home."

I smile. "Okay, little dude. You get to help me finish your laundry."

"Okay."

Chapter Eight

Ox

Who the fuck would run Nero off the road to steal our shit? Who would have the balls to do it?

The ambulance is blocking the street as I pull up on my bike. Fat Cat and Big Ben are the only brothers at the scene right now. The others must have taken off to try and get the son of a bitch who tried to kill my brother.

"What the fuck happened?" I demand as soon as I hop off my bike.

A couple of police officers are standing guard around the scene but I don't even pay attention to them. I'm too busy trying to get to the bottom of what happened.

Big Ben nods at one of the cops who is standing guard. I see a pickup truck off the side in a jacked position with a smear of black paint on it. That must be the rat mother fucker who did this.

I see a man standing next to it with his hands cuffed around his back. He's crying a little as if that would help him.

Nothing is going to help this sorry bastard by the time I'm done with him.

"That fucker rammed into Nero's back tire of his bike causing him to fall over," Big Ben explains with his teeth gritted.

Big Ben just did five years on the inside for some bull shit charge of killing The Pope, a rival president to another biker club. I have a feeling the only reason why he hasn't shot the asshole is that he doesn't want his parole to be yanked.

Me not giving a fuck, I charge at the man in the handcuffs. "I can't wait for you to be released," I seethe.

I don't need to get arrested especially since I just got my son. He doesn't need to have a deadbeat dad as I had.

"Ox!" Fat Cat yells.

I take a step back from the sorry worthless piece of shit that is going to get killed on the inside. "What?"

That's when I see it.

They are picking Nero up in a black bag to put him in the back of the ambulance. I want to yell and I want to kill someone for killing my brother.

Big Ben yells and tries to push over the EMT who is closing the door. "You have to save him!"

"Sir, your friend-"

"Brother. He's our brother," Fat Cat interjects.

"Your brother lost too much blood. I'm very sorry for your loss."

I take a look at the guy who is handcuffed and punch him in the face then punch him in the gut. He falls to the ground in pain. I kick him in his back twice before hearing a rib break.

"Ben, I'm warning you! You gotta get your men in line!" One of the police officers calls out behind me.

I don't care.

It isn't until I feel hands trying to pull me away from the man do I register what happened.

My brother died.

The shipment can wait for another day. I will deal with that another time.

Fat Cat, Big Ben and I jump on our bikes to follow the ambulance to the hospital. Nero deserves that much after being killed so recklessly.

Nero would have done anything for us. He was the best brother out there and I'm going to hunt whoever called this move down.

I have this niggling feeling in the back of my mind this is connected to Big Ben's arrest five years ago. I know he said The Cobras were the ones who framed him and we haven't had a chance to retaliate just yet.

This must have been their move to get us on our knees.

Once Nero has been taken inside, Ben is calling Skip, one of the older brothers who must have been riding with Nero to drop off the shipment, to see where they are.

He answers quickly. I can hear how loud he is through the phone. "We're over in Potter's Park. Near the dump."

The look Big Ben gives both of us is enough for us to immediately rev our bikes to go to Potter's Park.

Potter's Park is the dirtiest part of our city. A lot of prostitutes hang out there, pimps are strolling the streets looking for new girls and then you have The Cobras MC located right in the middle of the park.

Cobras are fucking worthless pieces of shit who try to take over all of our money-making venues. I wouldn't be surprised if they have taken hookers from the park and started pimping them out. That is something those desperate assholes would do.

The thing I don't like about Potter's Park is the fact it is run by a local gang. The Park Boys started in the state prison and spread out into the streets a few years ago. They have managed to push out the other rival gangs to make the property their own.

I haven't had any run-ins with The Park Boys, and today isn't the day for that to change. I'm feeling like I'm about to lose control.

I can see the line of bikes outside of a bar with the Saint Bastards MC logos on all of them. It looks like our brothers found the assholes who killed Nero.

I don't want to wait for Big Ben to decide on what we're going to do, but I do it anyway. I don't need to be on the receiving end of his beat down today.

"What's goin' on here?" I ask while jumping off my bike.

From what I can see, six of our brothers are surrounding three people outside of The Park Boys den. The three people have their guns out and look like they are about to shoot.

What I can see behind them is the duffle bag of our cocaine that had been sold.

I'm gearing up to run after it when Ben holds his hand up to stop me.

"Are these the fuckers who stole from us?" His words are like daggers.

Skip nods. "Yeah. We caught up to them when they were trying to pull the products inside."

Jack asses. These guys must have a death wish.

"Where are the others?" I ask.

Just like cockroaches, where there are three, there are six.

A couple of more guys come out of the dilapidated shack behind us with their guns trained at us.

I pull mine out and shoot the younger gangster right between the eyes. He falls instantly.

My move is what started the next events.

The war between The Park Boys and Saint Bastards MC has just begun.

One of the gangsters comes up behind me and punches me in the back of the head, I turn around and push him to the ground. I place my foot on top of his head to crush his skull against the concrete.

His skull makes a satisfying cracking noise.

I kick him one more time to make sure he's dead.

The next guy who comes up to me cuts my arm with a sharp knife. I feel the blade pierce my skin ever so slightly.

I shoot him quickly. I don't need him getting a bigger knife.

With my gun raised, I fire three bullets at the guy who has his own gun raised at Big Ben. He drops to the ground.

In the distance, I can hear the sirens go off.

"Grab the shit and let's go!" I yell. I'm running towards the duffle bag when I feel someone punch me in the back. It is a punch that almost knocks the air out of me.

I have the duffle bag around my arm as I run back to my bike. All of my brothers hop onto theirs.

We're off before the sirens catch up and grab us. That is the last thing we need right now.

By the time we get back to the clubhouse, I'm spent. I'm also ready to grab one of those gangsters and squeeze him for information.

"What the fuck, Ox?"

"Why do you live like you have extra lives?" Skip yells once we park.

I shake them off while dropping the bag onto the ground. "I gotta go," I mutter.

My mind is focused on getting home before I punch one of these assholes for pissing me off.

It is true, though. I think about how I live and the way I handle myself all the way back to my house. I have lived a rougher life and don't really care about what happens to me. I have never been the careful type, and I don't plan to be.

In fact, it wasn't until I found out about Callum did I realize I have something to live for.

I park my bike off to the side of the cages. I know I need to apologize to Tia for making her stay so long to watch Callum. I never would have thought I would be saying goodbye to a brother of mine.

It's rough saying goodbye to anyone, but Nero didn't deserve this.

Entering my home, I'm met with something I never expect I wanted. I never expected I would want a woman waiting for me at home with my son.

Tia is on the couch with Callum resting on her stomach. She looks comfortable. She looks like she belongs here.

Quickly pulling off my boots, I make my way to my bathroom to get rid of everything that happened today. I'm needing to forget for a moment what happened today.

I shed my clothes in my room with the door cracked open when I hear little footsteps approaching me. I'm only in my briefs as I turn to see Tia at the door.

"Ohmigod. Are you okay?"

Chapter Nine

Tia

As natural as breathing, I rush over to Brandon to make sure he is okay. Brandon is covered in bruises but it is the pain in his eyes that gets me.

"Tia, I'm fine," he mutters with his eyes directly on me.

He looks the opposite of fine. "Do you want me to go?" I'm standing directly next to him with my hand resting on his shoulder.

Brandon shakes his head then turns into my touch. "I don't want you to leave," he mutters once again.

"What happened?" I whisper.

"I don't wanna talk about it."

I half-smile in an attempt to ease the tension in the room. I'm so confused as to why I'm still here. I don't understand it.

But it is the most natural thing ever to be here with Brandon and Callum.

"Let's get you into the shower to wash you off," I suggest.

His eyes are haunted when they reach mine. "You've been here for a night and you're already bossing me around? Or is it because you wanna see me naked?"

The way his smile dances on those full lips as me stripping out of my clothes and reaching around him to start the water in the shower. I wiggle my fingers in the spray stupidly waiting for it to heat up.

I feel the heat of Brandon behind me as I do it. His hands splay on my stomach and I moan. I haven't been touched in a long time besides myself. My job makes dating a little tricky.

Involuntarily, I move my bottom to rub against his groin. His fingers spread over my abdomen then brush against where I need him the most.

I'm feeling out of control. I'm feeling something I never expected I could feel.

"Are you sure about this?" He whispers against my ear.

I nod. "Definitely."

Brandon picks me up around the waist quickly and my legs band around him. He pulls back the shower door then walks inside. My back is pushed up to the cold shower walls.

"You're so sexy," Brandon mumbles on my lips.

He's blocking the spray from hitting me with his big body.

"Kiss me," I beg.

His lips take mine completely; he kisses me like a hungry man. Our tongues begin their own erotic dance in the middle of our mouths and I feel his dick hitting my opening.

I wiggle a little to get him to push inside of me. His cock is the biggest I have ever seen and he stretches me completely. My lower stomach muscles pang with the excitement of the delicious stretch.

He quickens his thrusting with his groin hitting my clit just right to have me spasm around him.

"You're fuckin' amazing," he chants.

I feel his thrusts speed up and then slow down with his heavy sac hitting my ass. I'm too close to coming to stop it.

"Jesus!" He moans against my neck as he follows behind me.

The after-sex high is something I'm not familiar with. I've been with a couple of men, but they have never made me orgasm this way. They have never made my whole body spasm to the point of losing myself like this.

I should feel embarrassed by how quickly I came or even how quickly I allowed him to have sex with me. I don't, though.

It is the strangest thing.

"Tia," Brandon whispers against my lips.

"I know. I felt it, too," I whisper back.

"I know it's crazy but..."

I smile against his lips. "Let's get you cleaned off and then..."

"Don't go tonight." The way he says it has my heart soaring.

"Okay."

*

He's cleaned off and I smell like his body wash. I would say that was a win for me.

Brandon throws me a long tee-shirt of his and I quickly put it on relishing the feels of the over-used cotton as it spills down my skin.

I'm grabbing my underwear when I feel his hand smack me on my ass.

"Don't put those on. Go on and get in my bed and I'll be back in a minute."

I follow directions without throwing him some sass for being so bossy. I have never been the type to be so compliant but I can't help it with him. I love how he makes me feel.

Damn, I love being in here.

Chapter Ten

Ox

Not only did Tia step up and help care for my son last night when I had to go, she washed all of Callum's clothes for me, and then stayed all night but when I wake up the next morning, I smell breakfast.

This woman is hands down the best fuckin' ol' lady.

Pulling on my boxers and throwing on a tee-shirt, I make my way to the kitchen.

"Do you how many letters are in the alphabet?" Callum asks Tia.

"Um, ten?"

He giggles. "No, you silly bob!"

"Twelve?"

I smell the bacon cooking in the oven and see the pancakes on the griddle on the counter.

"Good morning," I greet.

"Dad! You're home!"

"I told you your dad was home," Tia replies happily.

I grab Callum by the waist since he runs towards me. "Good morning, little dude. How'd you sleep?"

"I did lots of sleepin'! Tia washed all of my clothes and we played with toys!"

"Tia's pretty great, huh?" I wink at Tia who is staring at me with wonder.

I place Callum down on the ground and then walk over to Tia. My hands grab her by the back of the neck to kiss her. She opens up to me immediately and I fight the urge to take her back to my room.

"Thanks for makin' breakfast," I tell her.

She smiles. "No problem. My work phone was ringing and then it woke Callum up. He said he wanted pancakes."

"You like pancakes that much?" I ask my son.

"Mom never made them for me. I got them one time from a restaurant and I loved them!"

I'm surprised how good his speech is after he went through so much with his mom. I wish Megan would have told me from the beginning that she was pregnant with my kid. I would have been there for them. I would have taken him earlier to help.

A boy needs his father.

My phone's ringing off to the side plugged into the wall. I glare at it for a second before answering it. I didn't want this feeling to be put on hold. This feeling of a family.

Callum's chatting happily with Tia and dousing his pancakes with enough syrup for my whole club while I answer the phone.

I'm not surprised to see if it Big Ben.

"Where are you?"

"Prez, what's goin' on?"

"I need you down at the clubhouse."

I look over at Tia and Callum eating breakfast together. My own breakfast is plated next to them at the breakfast bar.

Everything seems so domesticated. It seems so unreal. Yet, I want it more than ever. This is what my son needs all along. This is what I needed but never expected I did.

"What happened?"

"We have shit to discuss. We're lockin' down. I need you now."

Tia and Callum are acting like they are the only ones in the room by laughing and dipping their fingers in the syrup.

"I'm not alone," I mutter.

He doesn't chuckle. He doesn't say anything besides: "I didn't ask if you're alone. I'm tellin' you to get your fuckin' ass here, now."

"Give me about an hour."

"Everything okay?" Tia asks.

I smile and sit down next to Callum to eat my breakfast. "Yeah."

I'm lying.

Chapter Eleven

Tia

I'm finishing breakfast and rinsing off the plates when Brandon pins me against the counter with his body. I smile and turn off the water. I'm cursing myself for how natural this feels. It shouldn't be this natural.

"I have to go back to the club. Get dressed. Callum, go brush your teeth and get dressed!"

Callum is buzzing with excitement. "Where are we going?"

"We're gonna go to my friends' house."

"Whoohoo! Can I bring my Gameboy?"

"Of course."

I turn in his arms and kiss him on the cheek. "I'm going to go," I whisper.

"I don't want you to go home. Get dressed. You're comin' with me."

I scoff. "Excuse me?"

He smiles at me wickedly. "I'm not gonna tell you again. Get some clothes on that sexy ass so we can go."

I shouldn't let him boss me around like this. I shouldn't let it be so exciting for me to be bossed around a man I let have sex with me last night and now I'm playing house with him.

What's wrong with me? I'm screwed up.

I leave the kitchen and go to his room to pull on my clothes from yesterday. I'm not excited about wearing the same clothes I wore yesterday but I'm excited to spend more time with Brandon and Callum.

I know we're playing house. I know this probably doesn't mean anything to him and I'm just another chick in his bed. However, I find myself wanting to risk it. I find myself wanting to risk my heart to be with him.

I'm leaning over to pull my pants on when I feel Brandon behind me again. His hands wrap around my waist and he's picking me off the ground. I fly gently across the room and land on the bed with a light thud.

He rips the pants off my ankles and tears off my underwear. He looks hungrily at my sex with a wicked smile on his face.

"You're fuckin' perfect."

His mouth closes around my clit hard and two of his fingers spread me open for him to get a better angle. I place my legs on either side of his shoulders to hold on.

I feel the pressure build up inside of my lower muscles as his tongue coaxes me to an orgasm. I place my hand over my mouth to stop the scream that is bubbling up.

Over and over, his tongue battles my clit then makes love to it slowly. He builds me up then lets me come down to drive me closer to the edge.

"Please, please!" I beg quietly against my hand.

He licks me quicker and bites down gently around my little bundle of nerves. I'm coming unglued and there there is nothing that can be done to stop it.

He kisses me one more time on my clit causing me to shake and shiver from pleasure.

"That was incredible," I breathe out. My heart is beating quickly inside of my chest. I can't stop my ragged breathing. He's the best.

He crawls between my legs and spreads my thighs with his hips. In an easy move, he's inside of me again. I reach behind me to grab a pillow to place over my mouth but he knocks it out of my hand.

"Jesus, what are you doin' to me?" He mutters with gritted teeth.

"I could ask you the same-oh, fuck!" I whine. He's hitting my special spot that has my legs spasming.

I'm coming again and this time I scratch my nails up his back. I grip down on his shoulders to meet him halfway with the thrusts.

In a quick move, Brandon has me flipped over to my side with my ass in the air. His hands spread on my hips then bite into the fleshy skin. He's thrusting inside of me again and this time I bite the sheets to stop myself from screaming.

"You're a fuckin' angel," he whistles while his balls hit my clit over and over again.

"I'm coming again!"

"Do it, baby. Come for me!"

I let go and I feel every neuron in my body spasm and shake from the sheer pleasure of my body.

He follows behind me.

Chapter Twelve

Ox

We're on our way to the clubhouse. Tia and Callum are following me in her cage while I'm on my bike speeding down to the clubhouse.

Our nooner made us late, but it doesn't matter. Tia is incredible.

I don't know what this means for me and I don't know what it means for Callum.

What I do know is the fact this truck has been following us for the last three miles. I have sped up and slowed down, turned left and then turned right. The truck has been there this whole time.

Fuck. We're being followed.

I'm looking behind me trying to think of what to do to get this truck off of Tia's ass. That's when I see the truck speed up and hit the bumper of her car hard enough for her to swerve a little.

I see red. I stop my bike quickly and pull out my gun to have it trained on the asshole who is trying to kill my woman and my son.

The guy in the truck speeds up and tries to hit me but I get out of the way quicker than they realize. I shoot the back tire of the truck and watch it swerve off in the distance.

I'm pulling my phone out of my cut pocket to call Big Ben and Fat Cat to tell them to get here now. First these fuckers kill my brother and are now trying to kill my woman and son?

I'm feeling murderous.

"Those fuckers tried to run me off the road! They hit the car with my woman and my son in it!" I yell down to Big Ben.

"Where are you?"

"About two miles from the clubhouse. Get here, now. Bring a cage. I need to go after them."

"I'll be there in a minute. Fat Cat! Skip, Bando, Kilo and Mike, we gotta go!"

The line goes dead and I'm standing in the middle of the road with a wide-eyed woman and my son.

I yank the car door open that has Callum inside and pull him out of his car seat. I hold him close to my chest while Tia comes out of the driver's side door.

"What happened?" She asks.

"Dad, is Tia okay?" Callum asks quietly.

"I'm okay, Callum," Tia whispers. "I'm okay. Are you okay?"

I walk with Callum over to Tia and pull her close to me as I hear the rumble of the bikes coming. I see the armored truck being driven by Fat Cat that we use to move products and we use to make sure people are safe.

Big Ben is rushing over to us and he's grabbing Tia away from me. "Are you okay, little darlin'?"

Tia's eyes meet mine and I can tell she's confused.

"We're all okay."

I nod my head to Fat Cat who is pulling Tia and Callum towards the armored truck to get them out of the way. I don't want Tia to hear what actually happened here. The last thing I want is for her to be afraid of me.

"It was The Park Boys. They are workin' with Cobras. I'm gonna kill them!"

Big Ben spent five years in prison after being framed by the Cobras. I know he has his own personal vendetta against them and is wanting to take them out himself. I have wanted to wipe them out ever since they started messing with the fences.

They need to stay in their lanes.

All of the brothers like to tell me I have a death wish, and that might be true. I might have one. However, I'm not the one that is going to be pushed around by these fuckers who think they can bully us.

"Who's the girl with you?" Skip asks.

"That's my woman, Tia. Don't let anything happen to her or my son!" I demand with my teeth clenched.

He nods. "We're gonna go back to the yard with them. Let me know if you need anything."

I see Tia's purse sitting in the front seat so I decide to grab it to make sure she gets it. I hand it over to Skip who chuckles.

"She already has you carryin' her purse, huh?"

I flip him off. "Whatever. Get them back safe."

Chapter Thirteen

Tia

How did I become this woman?

The woman who is walking into a den of people that have no idea who I am and I have no idea who any of them are. Much less, walking in with a child that is not even mine.

When I became a social worker, I vowed to care for the kids in my care. I truly stand by that. I just didn't think I would be sitting here in a place full of people I don't even know like this.

Kendra comes straight towards me with a smile on her face. "Tia! Welcome!"

I smile back at her. "I don't know why I'm here," I whisper. It's the truth. I have no idea why I am here. This isn't the kind of place I would even come to.

"You're here because Ox really cares about you and wants to keep you safe," she mumbles and drags me through the clubhouse.

The friend that she was talking to stands up to say hi. "I'm Amanda. I'm Kendra's best friend."

"I'm Callum," Callum whistles at the pretty girls.

He bats his eyes at Amanda and then winks at her.

"Oh yeah. He's definitely Ox's son."

"Does this happen a lot?" I ask.

Both of the girls shrug. "Let's get Callum set up in the kitchen with a snack!" Amanda suggests wiggling her eyebrows at him.

He giggles while dropping my hand like a hot potato to run over to Amanda. He doesn't even look back at me as he leaves.

"Why do you call Brandon Ox?"

Kendra giggles and rubs her stomach. "I guess because he's as stubborn as one."

"I could see that."

She plops back down on the couch and pats the cushion next to her. "It's probably going to be a long day. You should get comfortable."

*

She wasn't kidding. I have been here for four hours and Callum has helped himself to all of the gaming systems in the clubhouse and endless snacks. He is now polishing off his third piece of cheese pizza with a cup of pop.

I think this kid is going to be happy here.

I can hear the rumbles of the motorcycles as they come back in. It sounds loud against the quiet house setting.

Kendra gets up to look out to see who is here and it's her face that makes me realize it's not our guys.

The front door is shot about fifty times and I can hear the bullets echoed off the metal door and bing against the windows.

I scream while I run to grab Callum. We are running behind the couch when the door opens suddenly. It crashes against the wall.

I place my hand over Callum's mouth so he doesn't scream. I don't want them to see us.

"Well, well, well. Looks like those motherfuckers left y'all alone," a gravelly voice calls out into the room.

Kendra and Amanda are running to a room in the back of the clubhouse as quickly as they can. I consider giving up my hiding spot, but I don't want to scare Callum even more than he is.

I hear the heavy boots hitting the ground as they round the couch. I shouldn't have hidden here. I'm stupid. I should have run with Kendra and Amanda so then I could have a chance.

I peek up to see a man wearing a similar leather vest as Brandon wears. He has his gun pointed at me.

"No," I beg. "Please not in front of the child," I try to shield Callum from looking.

Callum has probably seen his fair share of violence in his past and I don't want to add this to it.

Callum lets out a light sob next to me. It's quiet, but I know he's afraid.

"It's going to be okay, sweetie," I whisper soothingly.

The gun is cocked and I wait for it to go off.

Chapter Fourteen

Ox

We are rolling up to The Park Boys compound in record time. The truck led us straight here which is great.

I'm ready to get this shit handled and get it done with. I'm tired of these bastards playing with us. Plus, they put my woman and Callum in danger.

One of their guys is hanging off to the porch with a proud smile on his face. "You would think you guys had enough. Just like cockroaches, you never die."

I have my gun aimed at his head in seconds. I don't care if he's not charging at us. I'm ready.

"You put my woman and my son in danger!" I yell.

Big Ben holds his hand out for me to stop. "What the Cobras offerin' you?"

"A lot more than you, fuckers."

I knew it.

"Did you help them frame me?" Ben asks the question he's been dying to know the answer to for over five years.

The guy smirks. "I don't know anything about that. What I do know is you killed some of my men and know I'm gonna kill your women."

"What did you say?" I ask.

Fat Cat jumps off his bike and is approaching the scene. Even though he's a bigger guy, the man can walk quietly. "What did you do?"

A few of the Cobras walk around the compound with their guns held up. One of them has his phone in his hand. On the phone is the camera feed with the men shooting up our front door.

This was a setup.

"This ends today," Big Ben demands. "Call your men off and I won't fuck you up."

The Cobra shrugs. "It really doesn't matter what you fuckin' do to me. I'm the one who has the advantage. See, I'm the one who is controllin' whether or not your little women survive the night."

I move my gun towards the guy with the camera feed. I have it trained to his head but he doesn't care. It doesn't surprise him in the least.

I've only been a father for two days. Two official days of being a father and I already have him in danger. I haven't had a woman in a long time because I couldn't keep them safe and this is proving it. I knew I shouldn't have let it happen.

My brain is being tugged in two different directions between honor and being with my woman and son.

If we leave here, we are taking the war with us to the clubhouse. That is the last thing we are wanting to do. None of us are wanting our women to become a sacrifice for this war.

"You have something I want," the Cobra explains.

Big Ben doesn't budge. He doesn't acknowledge that the asshole has even said anything. Big Ben can be a soulless bastard sometimes.

"I want the fences."

I chuckle in the back of my throat. I'm watching the camera feed as the door bursts open and I see Kendra and Amanda running down the hallway into the president's room. I know he has a safe room in there and that is where she had been directed to go should this happen.

I'm looking for Tia and Callum but I can't see them.

"Do it," the Cobra says into his phone.

That is when he directs it straight to me.

"I take it you know these people?"

Fuck this. That's my son. That's my woman. I need to be there.

"Skip and Kilo, stay here!" Big Ben yells then jumps on his bike.

I'm following him and so is Fat Cat. I need to get to my woman and my son before that asshole finds them.

This is why war with these mother fuckers always turns bad. They take it too far and then we have to wipe them off the map. I meant it when I said this is why I don't take women in like this.

I would be my own soulless bastard because I couldn't keep my woman safe.

There is something in the way Tia looks at me with trust that has me rushing towards the clubhouse. She looked at me with sheer utter trust when I told her to get in the fan to go to the clubhouse. She didn't question me and she didn't seem like she had second thoughts.

The damage to the door is evident the minute we get to the clubhouse. I can see a line of the Cobras' bikes outside of our clubhouse and that is enough to piss me off even more.

I hop off my bike and run towards the side shed. Big Ben and Fat Cat are running inside to care of the assholes inside. I trust my brothers to care for my people.

I'm grabbing out a can of gasoline and the set of matches off to the side. Running out of the shed, I kick the Cobras' bikes over and watch them fall quickly. I douse them with gasoline and then strike the match. The matchbook is then dropped onto the pile causing the bikes to go up in flames.

Once the bikes have been torched, I'm running back into the clubhouse to get my woman and my son. I need to make sure they are okay. I need to get them into the back where the safe room is.

"Go to the back bedroom and knock on the door three times," Big Ben yells at Tia.

Tia is grabbing Callum's hand and pulling him down the hallway without a backward glance at me. I can't believe it has only been two days and I'm already thinking of her as mine.

When did I become such a pussy? I have no idea. I like it.

Big Ben has the man on the floor in seconds with his foot on his chest. "Tell me right now why you framed me!"

The guy is trying to wheeze out what happened but isn't able to say anything. Another man is barrelling around the corner and I shoot him.

I don't want any more of these assholes in our club.

"How many more of you are here?" I demand with sick satisfaction. I burned ten bikes. Ten bikes of these assholes who tried to kill my son and woman.

Ten bikes of these assholes who killed Nero.

Another man comes around the corner with his hands up. "You can kill us all. You don't know what they want, though. We're workin' for someone higher."

He takes his own gun in his cut and places it under his chin. It's quick. He falls to the ground in a thud.

"Jesus. Who are they workin' for?" I demand.

The guy below Big Ben's foot punches the president in the shin. Ben lifts his foot up so the guy can talk.

"What?"

"I can't tell you here. Act like you shot me and I'll tell you what I know."

Ben raises an eyebrow. I can tell he's considering his options but the truth is, can we trust this asshole.

Ben aims his gun towards the couch and shoots it. "Get him out of here."

I'm pulling up the asshole by his arm to yank him towards a room in the back so none of his friends can see him because he would get shot.

Sure enough, when I'm rounding the corner, I see a dark shadow coming out of the room I have here. He has a gun aimed at the traitor. The traitor drops then his gun is on me. I push him towards the door to knock the gun out of his hand but it falls to the ground. The gun fell just right for it to hit me in the leg.

I yelp out from being shot before leaning down and grabbing the gun from him. I shoot him twice in the head for good measure.

"Ox, you okay?" Fat Cat asks.

"I got knicked, but I'm okay. Let's get our people out and smoke out the rest of these assholes."

Ben is already down the hall opening his safe room. I can hear him fussing over Kendra just quietly enough for him to think we can't hear him.

Amanda comes running out of the room and straight into Fat Cat's arms. That's a new development. I didn't know those two were close like that.

I feel the blood oozing out of my leg. "Get doc here," I ask the brothers that have come in through the door.

I wonder what happened, but I don't ask. The last thing I remember is seeing Tia's scared eyes looking at me as I fall to the ground.

Chapter Fifteen

Tia

I'm not dumb. I know Callum and I could have easily been killed just now I know it could have happened and I wouldn't have been able to save him.

I'm sprinting out of the safe room with Callum's hand firmly grasped in mine. I see Brandon leaning against the doorframe with his leg slightly away from him.

"Is my dad going to be okay?" Callum asks.

I smile. "Yeah, he's going to be fine! Let's go see him."

Just as I say it, Brandon falls to the ground.

I'm rushing towards him to make sure he's okay when Ben turns to look at me. He shakes his head and points back to his room for Callum and I to go back inside.

I've done my best to be supportive this whole time, but I'm tired of these men bossing me around.

"I'm checking on Brandon!" I yell at him.

Ben's eyes shine bright with laughter. "You do have some spunk in you, don't you."

I nod. "Yep. Out of my way!"

Since Brandon's head is against the wall, I lean down to kiss him nicely on the mouth. He stirs a little but doesn't say anything.

Thirty minutes later, the doctor has stitched Brandon up and Brandon's up and talking. He's watching me interact with everyone including his son. Callum is loving all of the attention he is getting here. He can't get enough.

"Is it always like this?" I ask him quietly.

He smirks. "Not usually."

A couple of his brothers are walking into the room with a grim look on their faces.

"Where's Kilo?" Big Ben asks.

The way the men are looking down tell me where he is.

He died.

"Prez, the war ain't over."

Thank you for reading! I wanted these stories to be a quick and delicious read for you. Stay tuned for Fat Cat's story and the box set with newly added scenes for all three stories.